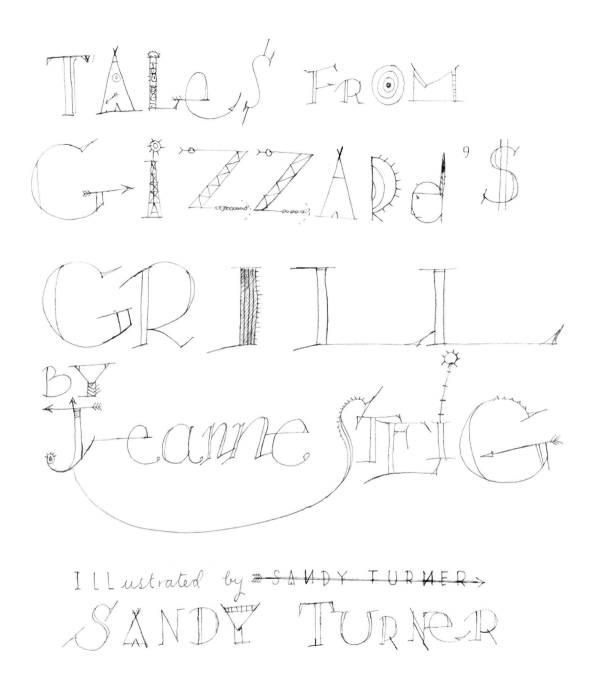

TALES FROM GIZZARD'S GRILL

BY Jeanne Steig

Illustrated by SANDY TURNER

SANDY TURNER

JOANNA COTLER BOOKS
An Imprint of HarperCollinsPublishers

Tales from Gizzard's Grill
Text copyright © 2004 by Jeanne Steig
Illustrations copyright © 2004 by Sandy Turner
Manufactured in China by South China Printing Company Ltd.

Library of Congress Cataloging-in-Publication Data
Steig, Jeanne.
  Tales from Gizzard's Grill / by Jeanne Steig ; illustrated by
Sandy Turner.— 1st ed.
     p.   cm.
Summary: Presents three tall tales from the Old West town of
Fiasco, where the lady sheriff keeps the peace, and friends, old
and new, enjoy the treats at Gizzard's Grill.
  ISBN 0-06-000959-4 — ISBN 0-06-000960-8 (lib. bdg.)
  [1. Frontier and pioneer life–West (U.S.)–Fiction. 2. Sheriffs–
Fiction. 3. Cowboys–Fiction. 4. Cowgirls–Fiction. 5. West (U.S.)–
Fiction. 6. Tall tales. 7. Stories in rhyme.]
I. Turner, Sandy, ill. II. Title.
  PZ8.3.S814Tal 2004
  [E]–dc21
                                                    2003006915

Typography by Alicia Mikles   1 2 3 4 5 6 7 8 9 10   ❖ First Edition

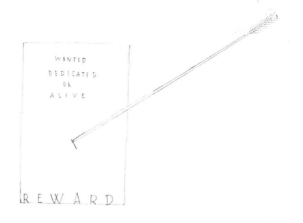

For Bill
—J.S.

For Christine Curry
-S.T.

☆ THE LONESOME COWBOY ☆

It was on an April morning,
'Bout a quarter after nine,
That the Sheriff spied a stranger man
A-sitting down to dine.

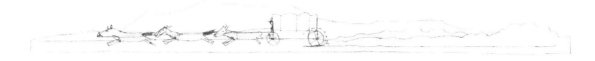

She moved in slow and easy,
Stepped over by his side.
"Now you know," said she, "there's just a few
Small things I can't abide.

"There's shootin', spittin', rustlin'.
There's gamblin', cussin', drink,
And I reckon I'd come up with more,
If I cared to stop and think.

"You see this badge I'm wearin'?
It ain't just foofaraw.
For in old Fiasco town, my boy,
I represent the Law."

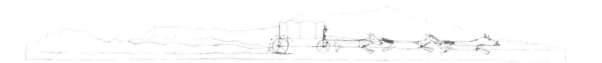

The stranger tipped his hat up.
He turned his head real slow.
When at last he spoke, his voice was soft,
And cold as mountain snow.

"I come here nice and peaceful.
I never tote a gun.
All I'm lookin' for in this here town
Is coffee and a bun.

"I am a Lonesome Cowboy,
I have no kith nor kin,
And the only man I care to know,
He occupies my skin."

Just then a great commotion
Resounded right outside,
And a rancher rushed in all distraught:
"Now I'll be skinned and fried!

"A horse-thief's grabbed my filly,
  And took off headin' east!"
  Well, the Sheriff jumped up and yelled,
"He'll get his carcass creased!"

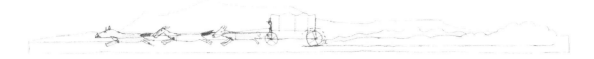

The townsfolk came a-running.
"We'll nab that low-down swine!"
And they saddled up and hit the trail—
But the Cowboy stayed behind.

They tracked him in the mountains,
They searched the flats and hills,
But they never caught that goldarn thief—
Though several men caught chills.

They rode back worn and dusty,
Dismounted with a groan;
And when every man limped home to bed,
The Sheriff rode alone.

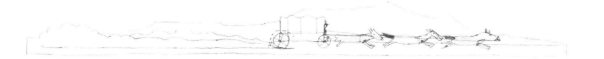

Through gullies, gulches, canyons,
She urged her weary steed;
When the trail dipped down she gazed around,
And stopped, surprised indeed.

There sat the Lonesome Cowboy,
As shoeless as a fly.
He had pitched his camp and hung his socks
Upon a branch to dry.

He'd stirred up stew and biscuits;
He hummed a wordless tune.
"I suppose you'll want a taste," said he.
"I hope you like raccoon."

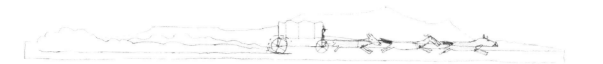

She hunkered down right grateful;
She sighed and stretched and smiled.
"The aroma of them biscuits there
Could drive a woman wild."

"I'm proud of these here biscuits.
I learned 'em from my gran.
They are made with stone-ground wheaten flour,
With just a touch of bran.

"There's one ingredient in 'em
I swore I'd never share,
If you chopped my toes in little bits
And fed 'em to a bear.

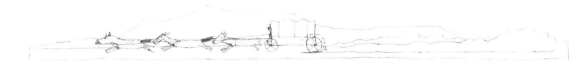

"But here's a little secret
 I learned when just a kid—
There's a cave way back in them thar hills
Where a horse-thief might be hid."

 The Sheriff whooped and hollered,
"Well, Cowboy, lead the way!
 We'll have that horse-thief roped and tied
Before the break of day."

 She grabbed a load of biscuits.
He pulled his old boots on.
Though his socks were damp, he never flinched;
Said he, "Ma'am, let's be gone."

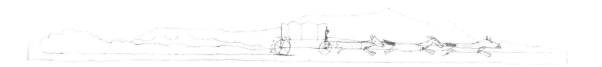

They rode a mighty distance
Before the sun rose up.
Said the cowboy, "Ain't come through these parts
Since Hector was a pup.

"Look there—them broken branches!
That varmint's passed this way;
He was steppin' out right hasty, too,
Upon his stolen gray."

The sky was wide and windswept,
With clouds like rags of lace,
When the Cowboy drew his horse up tight
And cried, "This here's the place."

The cave lay dark and dreadful,
And smothered deep in brush;

DARK AND DREADFUL

But that Cowboy's eyes, they pierced inside,
His face was all a-flush.

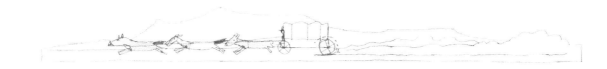

"I used to come here often.
I came with my true love,
And I vowed I never would return
Without my turtledove.

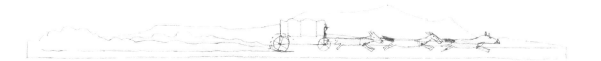

"She left me for another.
 She never said good-bye.
 Guess I'll be a Lonesome Cowboy now,
 Until the day I die."

"And that day's comin' fast, sir!
 You don't have long to wait!"
'Twas the hidden horse-thief's voice rang out—
 As sharp and sure as fate:

"My grandpaw was vexatious;
 My paw was meaner yet.
 I'm a terror when I'm hungry, and
 It's five days since I et."

Well, the Sheriff started shooting;
She aimed to either side,
And the little buds flew off the trees.
"I Am The Law!" she cried.

"Now you can dine on biscuits,
  Or you can dine on lead,
  For I'm comin' in to feed you now."
  (Those were the words she said.)

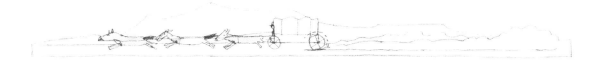

"Rein in your horse, dear Sheriff."
  (The thief it was who spoke.)
"I'm afeard you took my words to heart,
  When I meant 'em for a joke."

He came out pale and trembling,
His knees were clanking loud,
And he reached his arms so high above,
They grazed a passing cloud.

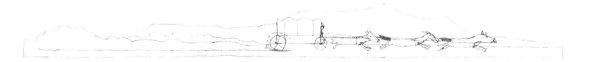

"My daddy was a barber,
  As gentle as a deer.
  If he chanced to nick a feller's jaw,
  He'd weep a thousand tears.

"My maw would bawl and blubber,
  To hear her boy went bad.
  I'd a whole lot rather eat that lead,
  Than make my mama sad.

"I am the worst durned horse-thief
  This land has ever known.
  I abominate the sight of blood—
  Especially my own.

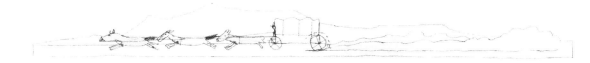

"I do repent my thievin',
 I loathe my life of crime.
 Why, the thought of livin' fair and square
 Sends a chill right down my spine."

The Sheriff glared down sternly.
"Where is that horse you stole?"
"She's a-restin' there inside the cave;
 I kept her good as gold."

He whistled for the filly.
She came at his command.
When he hugged her tight, she nickered soft;
You could tell she liked the man.

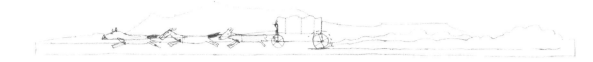

"Now saddle up and mount her;
You're gettin' one last ride.
If you try to tell us fare-thee-well,
I'll punctuate your hide."

They were pretty near starvation
When they got to Gizzard's Grill.
Not a word was spoke but "Pass that ham,"
Till the Sheriff paid the bill.

She wiped her lips and fingers,
She dabbled at her chin,
And her prisoner waited trembling till
She loosed a mighty grin.

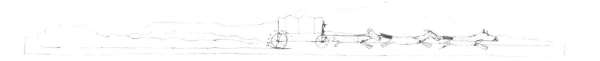

"I seem a tough old sheriff,
  Two-fisted, coarse, and hard;
  But beneath it all—you guessed it, boys—
  I'm soft as melted lard.

"I see you are repentant—
  That thievin's just a quirk.
  You can make your home right here in town,
  And get some honest work."

  Up spoke the Lonesome Cowboy,
"I guess I'll stay as well.
  Maybe build a little bake house here—
  Them biscuits sure would sell.

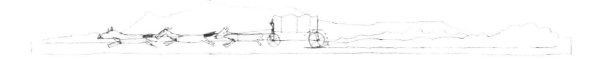

"I'm tired of witless wanderin',
 Of livin' at loose ends;
 And it seems I ain't so lonesome now,
 For I've got a pair of friends."

 The ex-thief choked a little;
 A tear stood in his eye.
"If there's one thing Mama learned me well,
 It's how to bake a pie.

"My crust is light and flaky,
 My fillin' is a jewel.
 If you'll let me share your oven, pal,
 I'll be a bakin' fool."

"I'm comin'," said the Sheriff,
"To watch them biscuits rise;
  And I'll be the first to whoop and shout
  For those dainty Horse-Thief pies!"

Miss Lou-Lou

"It's awful," groaned Louisa,
"The kind of appetite
  You can get from ridin' all day long
  Without one lonesome bite.

"And ain't this wagon creaky!
 And ain't my bottom sore!
 Do you think we'll get to some place soon
 Where we ain't been before?"

 Min gave a weary whinny,
 She tottered 'round the curve,
 Where a sign proclaimed FIASCO TOWN.
 Said Daddy, "This will serve.

"Fiasco's right good-lookin',
 And here's a smart hotel."
"It's the Fountain View," Louisa cried.
"Now doesn't that sound swell!"

The rent was next to nothing—
Exactly what they'd got.
"I've a crazy notion," Lou-Lou said,
"This is our lucky spot!"

"Ah, Lou, you're always dreamin'
We'll find some sweet abode.
But we've got no way to earn our keep;
We're doomed to ride the road.

"Let's wash up nice and pretty—"
"Alas," sighed she, "I fear
That the Fountain View is dry as salt.
There ain't no water here.

"No water in the pitcher;
 Ain't nothin' in the bowl.
 If you can't see why this room's so cheap,
 You're blinder than a mole."

"Dadrat it," growled her daddy,
"We're dirty as a hawg.
 You could almost say we're hardly fit
 To scratch a flea-bit dawg.

"Though we're a shame to look at,
 Let's have ourselves a meal.
 It'll cheer us up to be with folks
 So tidy and genteel."

But in Gizzard's Grill that evening
The folks was all downcast,
And they looked so pained it made you think
This meal might be their last.

They ordered up some victuals,
And Daddy gazed around.
"Well, it's just about as much fun here
As bein' hanged or drowned.

"How come," he asked the waitress,
"You're all so doggone grim?
I ain't never seen a place this bleak
Since we buried Cousin Jim."

"We've got us a disaster,"
She mournfully observed,
"And it's put us in a dreadful state,
Dejected and unnerved.

"I guess you're not acquainted
  With the news from Fountain View?"
"We ain't heard a thing," Louisa said,
  While tasting of her stew.

"The well," declared the waitress,
"That used to flow so free,
  Why, it's turned as dry as desert sand."
  The father said, "Ah, me."

"You're not a dowser, are you?"
"My foot don't fit that shoe.
  I'm a travelin', healin' sort of man—
  And entertainin', too."

"I need a bit of healin',"
  The waitress then replied,
"For my heart's been broke to smithereens.
  I longed to be a bride.

"The man I loved and trusted,
  That man, he did me wrong.
  Ran away one night with a light-o'-love,
  And took my heart along.

"His lover was a teacher
  Of music and of dance.
  When my man aspired to learn the waltz,
  She learned him hot romance.

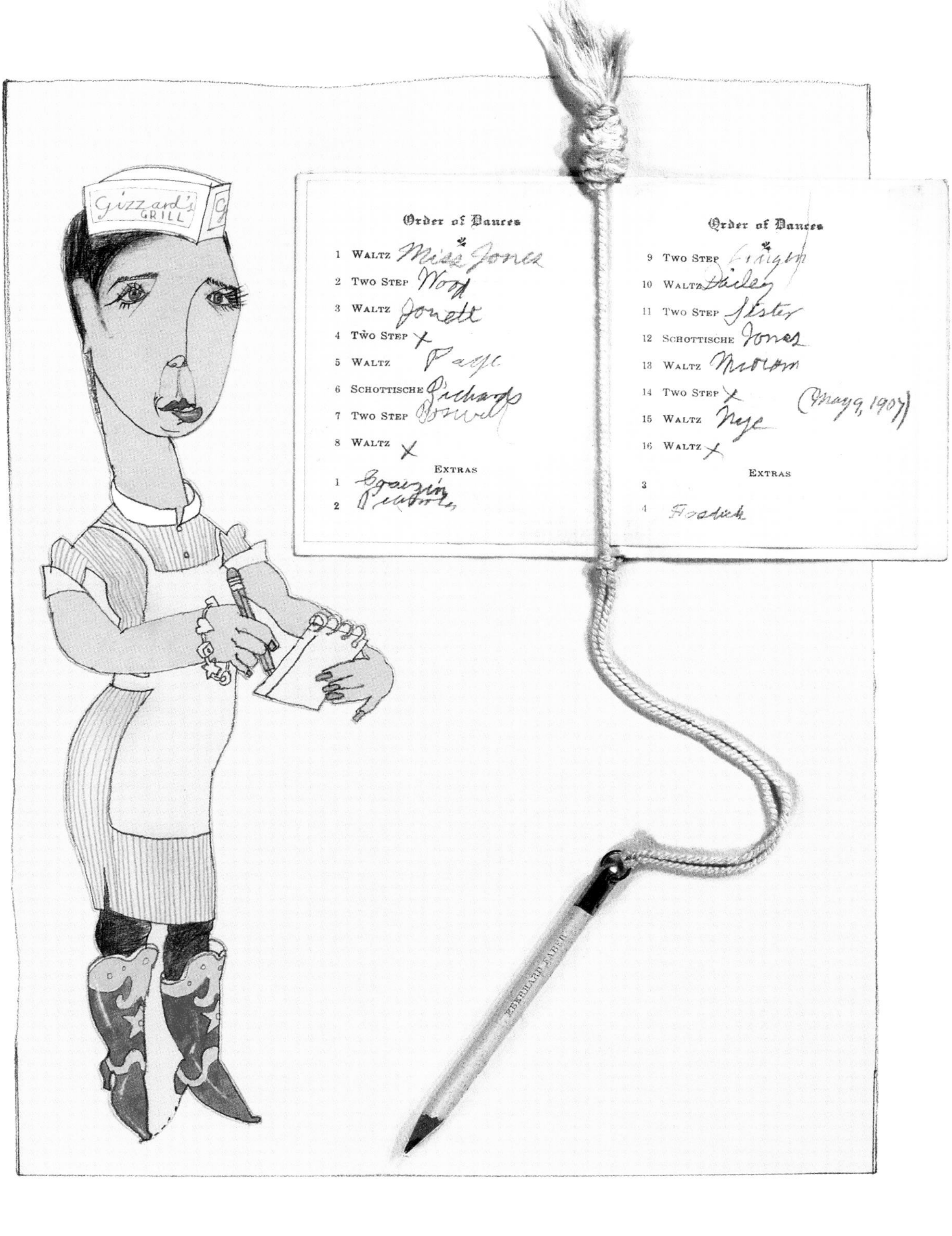

Gizzard's GRILL
Order of Dances
1 WALTZ Miss Jones
2 TWO STEP
3 WALTZ
4 TWO STEP
5 WALTZ
6 SCHOTTISCHE
7 TWO STEP
8 WALTZ
EXTRAS
1
2
Order of Dances
9 TWO STEP
10 WALTZ
11 TWO STEP
12 SCHOTTISCHE Jones
13 WALTZ
14 TWO STEP
15 WALTZ
16 WALTZ
(May 9, 1907)
EXTRAS
3
4 Fosdick
EBERHARD FABER

"I see you've finished dining.
 Would you like a slab of pie?
'Twas the former horse-thief baked it up;
 It'll make you want to cry."

 They chose the yellow custard,
 A fluffy lemon cloud.
"Now, whoever baked that thing," said Lou,
"His mama must be proud.

"I haven't got a mama.
 She died three years ago;
 So I ride the wagon with my dad,
 And help him with his show."

"Aw, that's a pity, honey.
  It's time to settle down.
  We're as friendly here as newborn pups,
  In old Fiasco town."

"Well, we're a wanderin' outfit,"
  Said Dad, "obliged to roam.
  Though if any place could do the trick,
  Fiasco'd be our home.

"The road was long and weary,
  We're worn clear down to shreds.
  But I hope you'll come tomorrow, miss,
  And watch my show," he said.

Their sleep was jarred next morning
By a hundred lunatics,
Who was rushing all around the place,
A-waving branchy sticks.

They dashed out in a panic;
The Sheriff yelled, "Join in!
There has got to be some water here
Where water's always been!"

"I ain't got no such talent,"
Said Daddy, "sad to say.
But I knew a lady, once, who did.
She'd a' found it right away."

He went to nail his notice
On every door and tree.
Little Lou-Lou took to looking strange.
"I see," she said. "I see."

She sped back to the wagon;
She dug around inside
Till she found a long tall package there,
All neatly wrapped and tied.

"My mother's gift!" she murmured.
"I never understood
 Why she left her daughter nothing more
 Than a wand of forkèd wood.

"A dowser's wand she gave me!
  She whispered, 'Darling Lou . . .'
Then she up and died, and left her child
Quite motherless and blue."

  She tore the wrapping from it,
  And raced to join the crowd.
"If there's water here, I'll find it fast!"
  The townsfolk laughed out loud.

"This child," exclaimed the waitress,
"This bird without a nest,
  Well, she's got herself a mean old stick—
  Let's put her to the test!"

Louisa got a-going,
She held her wand out straight,
And she moved deep back inside her head,
Where she could concentrate.

She combed the flower garden.
She searched beside the pond.
She inspected underneath the porch.
Her stick did not respond.

But when she turned the corner,
The thing began to pull,
And it dragged her toward a willow tree,
Where it bucked just like a bull.

An old, old man who sat there,
Declared the spot was his.
"I can hardly move from this here chair—
I got the rheumatiz."

A crowd of folks had followed,
To watch Louisa search.
Now the Cowboy pushed his way up front:
Said, "Easy, Mr. Lurch.

"I've heard it said that dampness
    Can ache you to the bone."
Then he picked the man right off his chair,
And perched him on a stone.

The wand was moving fiercely;
    It stabbed the ground below.
And Louisa, almost upside down,
Cried, "Here's the place, I know!

"Please, someone, start a-diggin',
    There's surely water nigh;
For my mama's wand goes straight and true,
It would not, could not, lie."

The men ran for their shovels,
They dug a mighty hole,

And the water welled up sweet and clear.
They hollered, "Bless your soul!"

"Ain't that a sight," said Lou-Lou.
"The water sure does flow!
 Now it's time, if you would be so kind,
 To see my daddy's show."

They stood before the wagon,
Her father smiled and bowed.
"It's a privilege to entertain
 This fine Fiasco crowd."

He did a little dancing,
He stepped out wondrous well,
And he sang a most melodious tune
Called "What I've Got to Sell."

"Now here's a rare concoction
  To soothe your every pain.
  It'll mollify your dandruff, ease
  Your gallstone, gout, and sprain,

"Eradicate your toothache,
  Your eczema, your grippe,
  It'll banish cramp and chilblains, piles,
  Lumbago, pukes, and pip—"

Up jumped the hotelkeeper.
"We've got just what we need.
  You can keep your rare elixir, man;
  Your daughter's done the deed!

"Louisa's found us water!
  So at the Fountain View
  There'll be room for free forevermore,
  To accommodate you two."

The waitress stepped up, smiling.
"You dance so well, and sing,
  You could be the music teacher here,
  If you'd like to try the thing."

"Miss Lou-Lou," said her father,
"You've made your wish come true.
  So I guess this *is* our lucky spot;
  We'll stay here, me and you.

"I'll be the music master,
  And you can go to school;
  And old Min can rest, and eat her fill,
  She'll be one happy mule."

The townsfolk cheered and hollered,
They threw their hats up high,
Then they all went back to Gizzard's Grill
For a slab of lemon pie.

THE DUEL

The crowd was feelin' festive
That day in Gizzard's Grill.
They had et real well, and hung around,
Not beggin' for the bill.

Then suddenly a stranger
Stood fillin' up the door,
And he sounded wild as ten wet cats
When he began to roar:

"Don't no one move a muscle,
Don't no one shoo a fly.
If there's one good man can put me down,
I'd love to see him try."

Up rose the valiant Sheriff;
She fixed her stern regard
On the wild intruder, and declared,
"Now, what's your trouble, pard?

"Fiasco is right kindly;
  We welcome strangers in.
  But before you start a mess down here,
  Just tell me who's your kin.

"I'd want to write 'em nicely,
  Explainin' how you died,
  At the Sheriff's hand, for makin' light
  Of our Fiasco pride."

"I'm here to raise this challenge:
  Bold townsfolk, if you dare,
  Just produce a man with feet like mine!
  It can't be done, I swear.

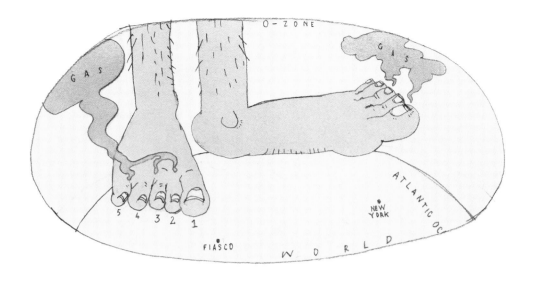

"My feet's a revelation,
And that's my guarantee.
They're the worstest smellin' pair of feet
On man or chimpanzee.

"I've roved the wild world over,
I've dueled with many a man,
And I've seen 'em all just laid out flat,
Like pullets in a pan."

"Well, here's one good old biddy
Can answer to your call!"
It was ancient Myrna Poke leaped up,
All wizened, weak, and small.

"I'm ready for a showdown,"
The little lady cried.
"Why, a passin' skunk once smelled my feet,
Flipped upside down, and died."

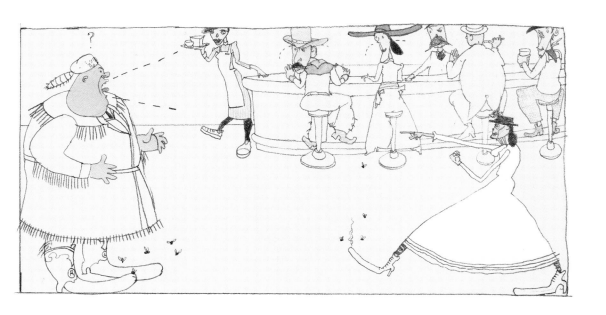

"I never," said the stranger,
"Have fought a female foe.
 From my head on down I am a gent—
 Not countin' foot and toe."

"Let's step outside," she hollered.
"Ain't nothin' to discuss.
 At the count of three we bare our feet,
 And see who bites the dust!"

Then out they strode together,
The door was bolted fast,
And the crowd peered through the windowpane,
To see which one would last.

The Sheriff called out loudly,
"A-one, a-two, a-three!"
Little Myrna flipped her shoe off fast;
The stranger's boot kicked free.

Point blank their feet were aimin'
Right at each other's nose,

And they yowled and gasped and each turned green,
And blue, and puce, and rose.

The very grass was withered,
Birds fell from rattlin' trees,
And they stood in clouds of fatal stink
That reached above their knees.

Miss Poke, she swayed and tottered,
Her lethal foot held straight,
While the stranger grabbed his throat and fell—
The man had met his fate.

"Bald bunions, I'm defeated!"
The shoeless stranger swore.
"And I know you beat me fair and square.
I ain't the champ no more."

"You fought me like a hero."
  Miss Myrna gasped for breath.
"Let's put on our shoes and step inside,
  Before we choke to death."

"Do tell us," said the Sheriff,
"Exactly how you came
  To possess such strangulatin' feet,
  Of everlastin' fame?"

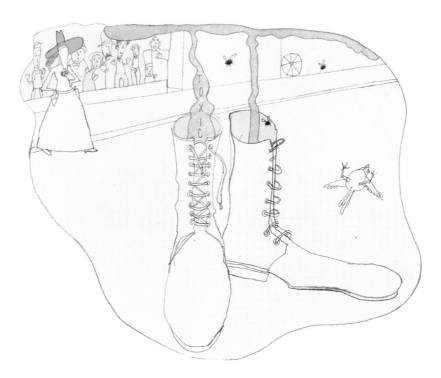

"My father," said the stranger,
"A man both wise and bold,
  He advised me not to wash my feet,
  To prevent the common cold.

"I've never had a sniffle,
  Ain't even blowed my nose;
  And I'd like to thank the old man, now,
  For what he did propose."

"My mama," Myrna answered,
"She made a lovely mix
  Out of rancid eggs and kerosene,
  To keep from gettin' sick.

"I've used it good and faithful;
 I never missed a day,
 And I'll tell you, folks, it can't be beat
 For keepin' colds away."

"Well, thank you," said the Sheriff,
"For that good ol' knock-down fight.
 You can stay in town, sir, if you wish;
 But keep them boots laced tight."

"I reckon I will stay, ma'am.
 No use to ramble on,
 For my record's broke by Myrna Poke;
 My glory days is gone.

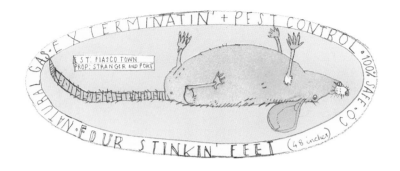

"I might suggest a business,
  If Myrna Poke agrees,
  Of exterminatin' roaches, rats,
  And cooties, worms, and fleas."

"I'm ready," cried the lady.
"We'll keep Fiasco sweet,
  There won't be a varmint left in town,
  With our four stinkin' feet!"